Guy Bass

AIDAN ABET TEACHER'S PET

With illustrations by
Steve May

Barrington Stoke

First published in 2016 in Great Britain by
Barrington Stoke Ltd
18 Walker Street, Edinburgh, EH3 7LP

www.barringtonstoke.co.uk

Text © 2016 Guy Bass
Illustrations © 2016 Steve May

A CIP catalogue record for this book is available
from the British Library upon request

ISBN: 978-1-78112-592-2

Printed in China by Leo

To my mum

CONTENTS

Chapter 1
The Unrelated Robinsons

"Aidan Abet, teacher's pet!
Peed his pants and now they're wet!"

The strange tale of Aidan Abet begins on the morning of the 5th of September. It was the first day of the new school term and Aidan was not looking forward to it for two reasons.

Reason 1 – The Unrelated Robinsons

Robert Robinson and Robin Robinson were unrelated but never seen apart, and so everyone called them the Unrelated Robinsons.

And the Unrelated Robinsons greeted Aidan Abet in the same way every day.

> *"Aidan Abet, teacher's pet!*
> *Peed his pants and now they're wet!"*

Every. Single. Day.

The Unrelated Robinsons didn't like Aidan. Aidan didn't like the Unrelated Robinsons. In Aidan's opinion, those boys were animals. And Aidan didn't like animals, either. Not at first, anyway.

Reason 2 – Mr Goodacre

Mr Goodacre was not a good teacher by any stretch of the imagination. He always looked like he was trying to remember where he'd left his car keys, or as if he had just smelled a fart. He was also lazy, and so Aidan employed the Assistance Approach with him. It went something like this ...

"Mr Goodacre," Aidan would say. "Would you like me to take the register?"

or

"Mr Goodacre, would you like me to collect in everyone's homework?"

or

"Mr Goodacre, would you like me to be dinner monitor so you can have a rest?"

Aidan knew that if he did Mr Goodacre's work for him, then Mr Goodacre would stop the Unrelated Robinsons from picking on Aidan. Of course, this meant everyone else in the class thought that Aidan was a teacher's pet.

The trouble was, Mr Goodacre had decided to retire at the end of the summer term. This was bad news for Aidan. Without Mr Goodacre to watch over him, the Unrelated Robinsons would pick on Aidan all the time. Aidan's only chance was to win over his new teacher as soon as possible and get the new teacher to put the Unrelated Robinsons back in their place.

So, back to the morning of the 5th of September.

"Aidan Abet, teacher's pet!
Peed his pants and now they're wet!"

As usual, those were the first words Aidan heard when he walked into the classroom on the first day of the new school term. He ignored the Unrelated Robinsons and the giggling from his classmates. He sat down at his desk, right at the front, and waited for the new teacher. He would do whatever it took to win them over.

He'd be keen but not *too* keen ...

He'd flatter them but not fawn over them ...

He'd be helpful but not smother them ...

Teachers were a predictable lot. Aidan had a plan in place for whatever the school threw at him. He was ready for anything.

But he wasn't ready for Miss Vowel.

Miss Vowel's application letter

Mr Headworthy
Teacup Lane Primary School
Teacup Lane
Spoonton
Stirshire SP23 OTL

Dear Mr Headworthy

I am writing to apply for the post of Year 6 teacher at Teacup Lane Primary School. I have more than five years' experience as a teacher. At ~~pheasant~~ present I am looking for a ~~pig~~ big challenge and I believe Teacup Lane would fit the bill. I am a team player who is willing to ~~pigeon~~ pitch in whenever I am needed. I'm well aware one must be able to wear many ~~cats~~ hats in this job and will take this ~~foal~~ role seriously. After all, the children's futures are at ~~snake~~ stake.

I hope to ~~deer~~ hear from you soon.

Yours sincerely
Miss Annabelle Vowel

Chapter 2
Animals

*"Animals remind us that the world
has an order to it.
Treat them as you would your fellow
classmates, only better."*

Miss Vowel walked in the door without so much as a glance at the children. She was short and lean with a sharp bob of brown hair. She wore a pair of oval glasses with thick blue rims and a plain brown suit. She looked like any other teacher.

But what followed her through the door made everyone in the class sit up.

Animals.

The school caretaker wheeled two large
trolleys into the classroom, crammed with
cages, hutches and glass tanks. All were
filled with animals. Aidan counted a rabbit,
a hamster, two gerbils, a turtle, three frogs,
newts and snails, and a green snake as long as
your arm, curled round a branch in a glass box.
By the time the caretaker had set the caged

creatures all in place around the edges of the
room, there were more animals than children.

Miss Vowel waited for the caretaker to
leave. At long last, she looked at the children.

"I am Miss Vowel and these are my
animals," she said. "Animals remind us that
the world has an order to it. Treat them like
you'd treat your fellow classmates, only better."

'Animals,' Aidan thought, with a shudder. 'Why did it have to be animals?'

Aidan didn't like animals for the same reason he didn't like his Aunty Pauline – they were strange, smelly and stupid. What's more, there was no way to flatter animals, so Aidan had no idea how to handle them.

Aidan sighed. 'Forget about the animals, focus on the teacher,' he told himself, and he put his hand in the air.

"Miss Vowel?" he said. "Would you like me to take the register? Mr Goodacre always got me to take the register."

Aidan ignored the groan from his classmates. 'Don't look back,' he thought. He pushed his arm a little higher.

"Miss Vowel?" he said again.

"I heard you," Miss Vowel said, without looking up. "Abet."

"I ... oh," Aidan said, and he put his hand down. He heard the Unrelated Robinsons snigger.

"Abet," Miss Vowel said again. "Abet."

"Yes, Miss?" Aidan replied.

"So you *are* present," Miss Vowel said, and she eyeballed him. "Then answer to your name when I say it. That's the point of the register, is it not?"

"Oh, I thought ... sorry," Aidan said. "I didn't know you were ..."

Miss Vowel went on with a tut.

"Bradman ... Chan ... Dhumal ..." she read out.

Aidan heard the Unrelated Robinsons laugh again, louder this time. If he didn't win over Miss Vowel fast, the Unrelated Robinsons would make his life a misery, for ever. He had to get a move on.

It was time to bring out the Big Guns.

Chapter 3
The Big Guns

"What now, Aidan?"

By lunchtime, Aidan had given it everything he'd got to win over Miss Vowel.

1. The Flattery Strategy

"Miss Vowel? If I had to wear glasses I'd want ones *just* like yours. They make you look so smart."

2. The Assistance Approach

"Miss Vowel? Do you want me to collect in everyone's homework?"

3. The Comparison Strategy

"Miss Vowel? You smell *so* much nicer than Mrs Underarm."

But Miss Vowel wasn't in the least bit interested. If anything, every new effort Aidan made seemed to annoy her more. She didn't even mind the other kids winding him up. The Unrelated Robinsons sang their 'Teacher's Pet' song three times that morning, each time louder than the last. Miss Vowel still didn't bat an eyelid.

Aidan's heart sank. The whole class was laughing at him. Even Ayesha Moon, who sat next to Aidan and was nice to everyone, let out an amused snort. And with every laugh, Aidan felt the world closing in on him, like the musty sour smell of Miss Vowel's animals.

The animals! Why didn't he think of it earlier?

"Miss Vowel?" he said, and he jabbed his hand in the air.

"What now, Aidan?" she replied with a sigh.

"Please can I help you look after your animals?" Aidan asked.

The whole class saw Miss Vowel's face change. All of a sudden she looked softer around the edges. "Why would you want to do that?" she asked. She sounded softer too.

"I – I just really like animals," Aidan lied, as he tried not to think about the smell. "I mean, I love them. I *love* animals to bits."

Aidan ignored his classmates' laughter. He focused on the warm smile that was spreading across Miss Vowel's face.

"You do?" she replied, and her eyes flashed.

And, just like that, Aidan Abet found himself a guardian to replace Mr Goodacre.

Chapter 4
The Zoo Keeper

"You're a good boy, Aidan."

For the next few days, Aidan spent every one
of his lunchtimes looking after Miss Vowel's
animals. He hated every minute of it. It wasn't
as if he had better things to do or had loads of
friends to hang out with – but all those animals
made his skin crawl. All that fur, all those
scales. And they went –

CHIRP!

CHIRRUP!

SssSSS!

whenever he came near.

Aidan felt like a zoo keeper – he was always tidying cages, filling water bowls or cleaning up poo. But Miss Vowel was happy to have someone – anyone – who cared about her precious animals as much as she did. She treated Aidan differently from the moment he became her animals' baby-sitter.

"You're a good boy, Aidan," Miss Vowel would say to him.

The more care that Aidan showed the animals, the more Miss Vowel seemed to like him. She even kept her eye on the Unrelated Robinsons. On more than one occasion she stopped the boys mid-song or chased them away from the classroom as they closed in on Aidan. So, every lunchtime, Aidan stayed in the classroom and looked after the animals.

Nothing could make him like them, but after a while the smell of them made him feel safe.

It was a Tuesday lunchtime, and Aidan was busy filling the water feeders for the rabbit, hamsters and gerbils. As he kept an eye out for the Unrelated Robinsons, he spotted the snake in its cage. It was pressed against one of the glass walls – but not in its usual squirming coils.

The shape of the snake formed a perfect "V".

"Huh," Aidan muttered. He edged closer. The snake didn't move, but it seemed to press itself harder against the glass. Aidan didn't know anything about snakes. Was this something they did? Did they make shapes? Could they make ... letters?

Aidan shook his head and shrugged it off. He checked on the other animals, to make sure they all had food and water.

He paused again at the snails' clear tank. The snails were as idle and disgusting as ever, with their glistening slime trails covering the mossy floor of their tank. For now they were still, except for the twitch of the long stalks above their eyes. But again, something odd caught Aidan's eye.

There was a slime trail along the wall of the tank. And when the light caught it just so, the trail looked like ... a human being.

It was a perfect human shape, with arms and legs and a head. And it was drawn by a snail with the slime from its single foot.

"No way," Aidan muttered. He stepped back. "What ...?"

He glanced around to check if someone was playing a trick on him ... but there was no one in the classroom. There was no one staring in at him from outside.

There were just the animals in their cages, staring at him.

The gerbils stared.

The hamsters stared.

The rabbit stared.

Then the rabbit flicked its head back. Again and again, like it was telling him to come closer. Aidan looked around again, and then he took a step forward ... and another, and another, until he was standing over the hutch. The rabbit edged into a corner, and Aidan peered inside. The floor of the hutch was full of droppings. Tiny black pellets peppered the sawdust-covered floor.

"I just cleaned you, you stupid thing." Aidan sighed. He glared at the rabbit in frustration. Then he did a double-take.

The rabbit's droppings had been ... arranged to spell out a word.

That word was HELP.

Chapter 5
Big Max

"Come and see me after school."

"How are my little darlings?" a voice said.

Aidan yelped as he spun around. Miss Vowel was standing behind him.

"They're ... look!" Aidan said, and he pointed at the cage. "Look at this!"

Miss Vowel peered into the rabbit's hutch.

"Oh, my!" she sighed. "It's *filthy*."

Aidan looked back at the cage.

A moment ago, the rabbit's droppings had spelled "HELP" in neat capital letters. Now there was just a mess. The droppings had been scattered everywhere.

"But ..." Aidan began.

"Aidan, you asked for this responsibility," Miss Vowel went on, with a look around the room. "Animals and silliness do not mix."

"But the animals – they're not – they're not normal! The snails ..."

Aidan pointed at the snail cage. Snails now covered the glass walls, their smears covering over any trace of a human shape drawn in slime.

"And the snake ..." Aidan added, and he spun around to the snake cage. But it no longer looked in the least bit like a "V". It had coiled itself around its branch, and it simply looked like a snake.

"But …" Aidan blurted again.

"Aidan, if you don't think you're up to this, you mustn't pretend you are," Miss Vowel said. "That's not fair on me, or you, or more importantly, the animals."

"I am!" Aidan said, in a sudden panic that he was about to fall out of favour with Miss Vowel. "I am up to it."

"That's good to hear," Miss Vowel said, and a smile appeared on her face. "I need to know that –"

A boy stumbled into the classroom, interrupting Miss Vowel mid-sentence. He was running so fast that he ran straight into Miss Vowel's desk and knocked a stack of text books onto the floor.

"Oops!" he said, trying to pretend he wasn't running in the first place.

It was Maxwell Small, the tallest boy in the class. Everyone called him Big Max. He was always crashing into things and causing a mess, and he always seemed to rather enjoy it.

Aidan was never one to miss a chance to keep his teacher sweet, and so right away he began to pick up the text books.

Miss Vowel stared at Big Max.

"It's still break time, Maxwell," she said. "Off you go, outside."

"OK," Big Max said, and he turned to go.

"And Maxwell," Miss Vowel added. "Come and see me after school."

Big Max shrugged and bumbled out of the classroom.

Aidan never saw Big Max again.

Chapter 6
The Register

"Another addition to the family."

A night's sleep will send you one of two ways –
you'll either dwell on your problems, or decide
to put them behind you. Aidan Abet decided on
the second course. He decided not to let all the
animal-related weirdness bother him. After all,
he still had another year of school to survive,
and that meant that the most important thing
was to keep Miss Vowel on his side.

"Aidan Abet! Teacher's pet!
Peed his pants and now they're wet!"

The Unrelated Robinsons were waiting for Aidan when he walked into the busy classroom. They sang at the top of their lungs, above the clamour of their classmates.

"Aidan Abet! Teacher's pet!
Peed his pants and now –"

"Robert and Robin Robinson," a voice said. From out of nowhere, there was Miss Vowel. She stood behind Aidan, as close as his own shadow. "If you want to sing, I'll sign you up for choir practice," she said to the Robinsons. "Would you like to join the school choir?"

The Unrelated Robinsons didn't answer. But they did stop singing. Aidan stifled a smile. Then he noticed that Miss Vowel was carrying something. She held it up high.

It was a bright blue and yellow parrot in a birdcage. Aidan shivered as the bird shuffled on its perch.

"Another addition to the family," Miss Vowel said, as the parrot let out an ugly *SQUAWK!* "Treat him as you'd treat your fellow classmates, only better. Aidan, will you keep an eye on him?"

"Yes, Miss Vowel," Aidan replied. He found birds even more unpleasant than snakes. But he was happy to have any chance to keep Miss Vowel on side. "Would you like me to take the register too, Miss?" he added. He didn't even put his hand up before he spoke.

Miss Vowel smiled. "You're a good boy, Aidan," she replied.

Aidan was half way through the register when he got to the Unrelated Robinsons.

"Robinson?" Aidan said.

"Here," Robert Robinson grunted.

"Robinson?" Aidan said again, with a smile.

"Here," Robin Robinson huffed.

They had to answer him.

Aidan would have done anything to bottle that moment. He returned to the register, as happy as he was going to be all day.

"Small?"

There was a pause.

Big Max didn't answer.

The parrot let out a *SQUAWK!*

"Small?" Aidan said again.

Another pause.

Another *SQUAWK!*

"Small?"

"He's not here," a voice hissed.

Aidan turned to see where the hiss had come from.

It was Serena Mint. She had a big mouth and big hair. Serena sat next to Big Max in class. Everyone said they were girlfriend-boyfriend.

"Here's not here," Serena hissed again, and she pointed at Big Max's empty desk. "Use your eyes ... Teacher's Pet."

There was a chuckle from the class. And a *SQUAWK!* from the parrot.

"Mark Maxwell Small as present, please, Aidan," said Miss Vowel.

"He isn't present! He's not here, I just told you," Serena snapped.

Miss Vowel looked Serena straight in the eye. Then she took off her glasses and slowly polished them.

"Serena, come and see me after school," she said.

Serena huffed and threw her hands up.

Aidan tried not to smile but he felt a smirk spread across his face. He felt invincible. For a moment, he wondered what Miss Vowel had said to Big Max after school. Maybe Big Max was too scared to come back.

Aidan shrugged, and he put Big Max out of his mind. In fact, he didn't think about Big Max until he next heard his name.

After that, he couldn't think about anyone or anything else.

Chapter 7
The Parrot

"SQUAWK!"

At lunchtime, as usual, Aidan stayed in the classroom to check on the animals.

Outside, in the playground, the Unrelated Robinsons pressed their faces against the classroom window and started to sing their song. But before they'd even finished the first verse, there was Miss Vowel again, looming over them. As she chased the boys away, Aidan looked over his empire ... his classroom of animals. Then the newest addition to his empire let out an almighty ...

SQUAWK!

"Squawk!" Aidan replied, and he turned to the parrot. He inspected its colourful feathers and its curved grey beak.

SQUAWK! SQUAWK!

"I thought parrots could talk," Aidan said. "You're all squawk, no talk."

Aidan turned away and headed for the rabbit's cage. For a moment, he wondered if he would see something written on the floor of its hutch, but no ... it was just the floor of a hutch. It almost felt as if he'd imagined the animal-related weirdness of the previous day.

SQUAWK!

"Squawk, squawk, squawk," Aidan sighed. "You really need to learn to –"

MAX!

Aidan froze.

MAX!

Aidan turned, as slowly as anyone has ever turned, to face the parrot. It swung from side to side, stepping to and fro in a frenzy on its perch.

MAX! MAX!

"What ...?" Aidan whispered.

MAX! the parrot squawked. *I AM MAX!*

Chapter 8
The Fate of Serena Mint

"My mum's waiting for me, Miss."

The parrot fell silent as the rest of the class hurried back into the classroom for afternoon lessons. Aidan remained frozen to the spot in the middle of the room. He just stared at the bird, struck dumb. He didn't even hear Robert and Robin Robinson singing their song. It wasn't until Miss Vowel entered and ushered him to his desk that Aidan sat down.

The rest of the day passed in a blur.

The parrot's words rang in Aidan's ears. What did they mean? Was there some link between Big Max and the bird? How did it know his name? Parrots liked to mimic – was it mimicking Big Max? In which case, had they somehow met? And where *was* Maxwell Small?

And then there was the darker mystery surrounding Miss Vowel's animals. The snake that had spelled out a "V" with its body ... the snail that had drawn a human shape in a trail of slime ... the rabbit that had spelled out "HELP" in its droppings. And now the parrot ... it seemed to think it *was* Maxwell Small! Aidan didn't know much about animal behaviour, but it all seemed so ... human.

Aidan looked behind him at Big Max's empty chair. He remembered how Miss Vowel had told Big Max to meet her after school. Now he was gone. Could there be a link? Aidan's eyes wandered over to Serena Mint. It was her turn to wait behind after school today.

Aidan's mind was racing. He couldn't believe he was thinking what he was thinking. But he couldn't deny what he'd seen.

He had to find out what was going on.

Two hours later, Miss Vowel dismissed the class as the bell rang for the end of the school day.

Only Miss Vowel and Serena Mint stayed behind. And Aidan Abet. Instead of walking home as normal, he made his way all the way around the back of the school. He hid for a few minutes behind the bins and then he headed round to the front of the school. He crossed the playground and edged towards the window of his classroom. It was open wide enough for him to hear what was happening. Open wide enough for him to clamber inside, if he dared.

But for the time being Aidan waited under the window, with no idea what to expect.

After a few moments, Aidan peered over the wall into the classroom – and found himself face to face with a parrot. The parrot opened its beak, but Aidan held a finger up to his lips.

"Shhhh ...!" he whispered.

The parrot cocked its head. It seemed to nod, as if it understood. It shuffled to one side on its perch so Aidan could get a closer look at what was happening.

He could see Serena Mint, sitting at the front of the classroom, looking more bored than anything else. Miss Vowel was behind her desk, stirring a strange red powder in a glass beaker. And then Serena Mint said –

"My mum's waiting for me, Miss."

"I'm sure she is," was Miss Vowel's reply. "But one day she will give up waiting for you. One day she will give up any hope of ever

seeing you again. And yet you will have been here, all along."

Her words were the second most sinister thing Aidan had ever heard. (The first most sinister thing was his Aunty Pauline calling their postman "a slice of cake I'd like to put in my fridge".) He saw Miss Vowel wave for Serena Mint to come towards her. Serena got up and edged towards Miss Vowel's desk. Aidan could tell that she was trying not to look scared.

"Do you like animals, Serena?" Miss Vowel asked. Serena Mint shrugged. Miss Vowel stood up suddenly. "Well, you had better start to like them!"

Miss Vowel dug her right hand into the beaker of red dust and flung a fistful of it at Serena. Serena coughed and stumbled back as the dust struck her. A second later, Serena Mint was ... transformed. The change was so sudden that Aidan would have missed it if he'd blinked. One moment Serena Mint was Serena Mint ...

And the next she was a gerbil.

"Aaah!"

Aidan screamed this time. It was loud and shrill, a howl of terror. As Miss Vowel bent down to pick Serena the gerbil up from the floor by her tail, she turned to see Aidan duck under the wall.

"Aidan?"

Aidan didn't answer.

He just ran.

Chapter 9
Maybe

"Bell's gone. School's done."

Aidan raced towards the school gate, his mind racing even faster. Miss Vowel had turned Serena Mint into a gerbil! And she must have turned Big Max into a parrot. Maybe all of the other animals in the classroom had once been children.

Aidan reached the gate and found it was locked.

Locked! And too high to climb.

Aidan doubled back and hurried around the other side of the school. If he could find a place to clamber through the back of the fence, maybe he could he get out of the school grounds. Maybe he'd be home in minutes. Maybe he'd tell his mum all about how Miss Vowel had turned Serena Mint into a gerbil and Big Max into a parrot and maybe his mum would call the police and maybe the police would call the army and maybe they'd all descend on the school and that would be that for Miss Vowel.

Maybe.

"Oi!"

Aidan skidded to a halt and spun around. He saw the back door of the school swing open. The caretaker leaned out.

"Oi!" he said again. "Bell's gone. School's done. What you still doing here?"

"Animals!" Aidan screamed. "She's turned them into animals! Have to go!"

"I'm not going nowhere until I finish locking up," the caretaker tutted, and he jangled the ring of keys on his belt. "And I'm not going to finish locking up with you running around like a headless chicken. C'mon, I'll let you out of the gate. Now where did I put that key?"

"I ..." Aidan began. He was still tempted to run, but he took a deep breath and did what he always did – focused on saving himself. The caretaker was his way out. Miss Vowel wasn't going to do to him what she did to Serena Mint with the caretaker around.

"Yes, sorry. I should go. I need to go," Aidan said. He edged towards the caretaker, looking left and right for any sign of Miss Vowel.

"Got it!" the caretaker said, as he brandished the gate key. He stepped out of the doorway into the playground. "Right then, let's get you out of –"

"Aaah!"

Aidan let out a scream. Miss Vowel was standing behind the caretaker.

"R – Run!" Aidan cried, but he was too late. Miss Vowel flung a handful of powder at the caretaker. Before he could even turn, he had been transformed. In a split second, there was no sign of the old man. Standing before Aidan was a huge, dark shape, three times Aidan's size ... a hulking mass of fur and teeth and claws. The creature let out a low, deep rumble, before it rose to its full height and cast a dark shadow over Aidan.

Miss Vowel had turned the caretaker into a *bear*.

Chapter 10
The Beartaker

"It's better if you don't run."

The bear fell onto its front paws in front of Aidan. It let out an angry snort, and Aidan felt its hot, wet breath on his face.

HRR HRR ...

Miss Vowel stepped back through the doorway into the school.

"It's better if you don't run – he'll kill you if you run," she said. "Of course, I imagine he'll kill you anyway."

With that, she shut the door.

For a brief, strange moment, Aidan wondered if the bear remembered it was a caretaker, just like the parrot seemed to remember it was once Big Max ... maybe it wouldn't want to kill him.

HRR ...!

But as he stared at the great brown beast, slavering and wild, Aidan decided not to risk it.

So he ran.

"Aaaah!" he screamed, as he raced across the playground away from the bear. Aidan looked back to see the bear pounding after him.

HRR HRR HRR ...

It was fast. Too fast. Aidan heard himself squeal in terror, felt his heart thump in his chest, heard his breath, shaky and desperate.

His instinct told him to weave back towards the school, away from the locked gate. But the school was locked too – Miss Vowel had seen to that. Aidan dared to look back one more time. The bear was gaining on him, and fast. He raced towards the school ...

Then he saw it.

The window to his classroom was still open.

Aidan headed straight for it, his legs moving so fast that he stumbled as he lunged for the window. He forced his arms under it and dragged the window open as far as it would go. As he heard the bear growl, he dragged himself up, squeezed himself through and landed on the window sill, knocking the parrot's cage onto the floor. Aidan tore his shirt on the window latch, tumbled onto the floor and landed with a painful thud.

HRR HRR ...!

He turned and saw the bear rear up and press its great clawed paws against the window, blocking out the light, steaming up the glass with its breath.

"Heeeellllp!" Aidan howled to a room that was empty except for animals.

MAX! I AM MAX! the parrot cried as its cage rolled across the floor.

Aidan scrambled towards the door on his hands and knees. He saw the gerbil that was once Serena Mint scurry across his path and under Miss Vowel's desk. The other animals began to cry out, squeaking and squawking and chirping and chirruping. He was almost at the door when he heard a

KRASSSH!

Aidan felt shattered glass rain down over his head. He turned to see the bear land awkwardly on the floor of the classroom. It

had broken through the window. Aidan tried to scramble to his feet as the bear shook its head in confusion. And, as it shook, it saw him.

HRRRR!

Chapter 11
Aidan's Gambit

"They still think like people."

Aidan reached for the door handle.

The bear lunged.

The door swung open ...

Straight into Aidan's face.

As Aidan fell backwards, dizzy from the sharp pain of the door slamming into his forehead, he saw Miss Vowel in the doorway. She'd thrown a handful of dust at the charging bear before Aidan even had time to hit the floor.

HRRR –!

In less than a second, that great brown bear had become a tiny grey mouse. It landed on the floor with a soft *thup* and then, after a moment of confusion, it scuttled away. Aidan held his bloody nose and stared up at Miss Vowel, wide-eyed with terror.

"Consider yourself lucky I have better things to do than cover up your death, Aidan Abet," Miss Vowel said with a shrug. "Consider yourself lucky I had a change of heart."

Aidan said, "Yes, Miss." He wasn't sure why, but in his terror he couldn't think of anything else to say.

"Disobedience has been the bane of my teaching career," Miss Vowel said with a deep sigh. "At first, I never knew how to keep my pupils in line. But then I realised that children – *people* – cannot be trusted to behave. Only a cage can ensure they remain under control. I knew then what I had to do."

"Yes, Miss," Aidan whimpered again. He could feel the warm blood trickle from his nose and between his fingers.

"As it turned out, I learned everything I needed to know about this from school text books," Miss Vowel said. *"Transmogrification!* The art of transforming one thing into another! It's all in there. Once I had discovered the secret of turning man into beast, I realised I could ensure good behaviour, without it affecting pupil attendance. After all, everyone is still technically in class … even if they're not altogether human. It's perfect! They're perfect!"

Miss Vowel dug her hand into the glass beaker.

"And now, I'm going to make *you* perfect, Aidan," she said.

"The animals are telling!" Aidan cried. "They're telling on you!"

Miss Vowel stopped and hovered over him with a handful of red dust.

"What do you mean, *telling*?" she asked.

"They – they told me what you did," Aidan told her. "The snake wrote 'V' and the snail drew you in slime and the rabbit spelled 'help' in poo! And Max ... I mean, the parrot! The animals ... They tried to tell me what you'd done ... what you were doing. They still think like people."

TEACHER'S PET! the parrot squawked from its upturned cage.

"Impossible!" Miss Vowel hissed. She glowered at the parrot and then her eyes

darted around the room, eyeballing each of the animals in turn with a look of rage. "Unless … could it be that their humanity is returning to them over time?"

"They wanted me to tell on you," Aidan said. "They wanted me to tell, but I didn't."

"Ungrateful creatures," Miss Vowel snarled. Her hand was still clutching the powder but it was shaking now. "I must be more careful, or else –"

"I can help you!" Aidan blurted. His mind raced. "I can make sure they don't tell! I can watch them for you. I can make sure they don't misbehave … But only if you don't change me."

TEACHER'S PET! the parrot cried. TEACHER'S PET!

"I'm not stupid, Aidan," Miss Vowel tutted. "If I let you remain as a human, you'll –"

"I won't! I won't tell! Not ever! I'll help you, I promise!" Aidan cried. He took a deep breath. "If ..."

"*If?* You're hardly in a position to bargain, Aidan." Miss Vowel laughed, and she held up her handful of dust. "If *what?*"

Aidan sat up and brushed the glass from the broken window off his uniform. He took a deep breath and narrowed his eyes.

"If you help me, too."

MISSING

Maxwell Small
(Sometimes called
"Big Max")

Missing – 12th September

Age – 11
Hair – Brown
Eyes – Blue

Maxwell was last seen on 12th September.
He was wearing a school uniform.
He is tall for his age.

If found, please return to –
11 Hunkerdown Hill
Spoonton
Stirshire SP23 0RG

Chapter 12
The Teacher's Pets

"Are they brothers?"

A week had passed since Aidan Abet was almost eaten by a bear. The shattered window had been explained away and replaced, and life had returned to normal.

It was Monday, and the morning sun that poured into the classroom was as bright as Aidan's mood. Life was good, school was fun, and the bullying had stopped altogether.

"Aidan, would you mind doing the honours?" Miss Vowel asked as she handed him the register.

"Yes, Miss," Aidan said. He made his way to his desk, which now stood out from all the rest. His desk was the only one with an animal cage sitting on top of it. He'd asked Miss Vowel permission to keep it there, so he could keep an eye on the classroom's newest pets.

Inside the cage on Aidan's desk were two small brown rats. Despite his dislike of animals, Aidan rarely let them out of his sight.

"Are they brothers?" asked Ayesha Moon, the girl who sat next to him.

"What?" Aidan asked, as he opened the register.

"The rats," Ayesha said. "Do you think they're brothers?"

Aidan Abet stared at the animals, and a smile spread across his face.

"No," he said. "They're unrelated."

Our books are tested
for children and young people by
children and young people.

Thanks to everyone who consulted on
a manuscript for their time and effort in
helping us to make our books better
for our readers.

If you enjoyed this crazy tale of animal antics, then you'll love ...

**Making cardboard elephants in class – BAD
Monkeys and meerkats in the playground – BAD
A new boy with a book allergy – TERRIBLE!**

The inspectors' report on Pudding Lane
Primary is pretty awful. And that's BEFORE
they meet Mad Iris ...

Whatever will they make of her?